D1388037

For Ivan

OLD Bear had been busy all morning. He'd packed an enormous picnic for all the toys. There were sandwiches, cakes, buns, pies and jellies.

'I think I've put in a bit too much food,' he said to himself as he sat on the picnic-basket lid to try to make it close.

Suddenly in a blur of fur and red trousers, Little Bear dashed past the basket and dived into a heap of books. 'Do you think anyone will find me?' he asked from the middle of the heap.

'I shouldn't think so,' said Old Bear. 'Who's looking for you?'

JANE HISSEY

Little Bear
Lost

HUTCHINSON
London Sydney Auckland Johannesburg

BUT before Little Bear could answer, the door flew open and into the room ran Bramwell Brown, Duck and Rabbit. They didn't seem to be looking for Little Bear and, in a moment, they were hiding too. Rabbit and Duck were behind the curtains and Bramwell's feet could just be seen sticking out from under a cushion.

'We're playing hide and seek,' explained the cushion in a Bramwell Brown sort of voice. 'Did anyone see us hide?'

'Only me,' said Old Bear, 'but who's looking for you?'

THERE was a bit of a silence and then the cushion moved.

Bramwell looked sadly up at Old Bear. 'Oh dear,' he said, miserably, 'we've done it again. We've forgotten to have a seeker in our game of hide-and-seek.'

The others crept out of their hiding places and sat down on Bramwell's cushion.

'What a pity,' said Duck. 'It could have been a good game, too.'

'Old Bear,' said Little Bear, thoughtfully, 'if we all hide again, could you look for us?'

OLD Bear said that was a good idea and, with paws over his eyes, he slowly counted to ten.

'One, two, three,' he began, as Rabbit jumped into a vase and tried to look like a bunch of flowers.

'Four, five, six,' he continued, as Duck jumped into a shoe box.

'Seven, eight, nine,' he said, giving Bramwell time to hide a last bit of paw.

'TEN,' he called; 'I'm READY!' And by then Little Bear had also disappeared.

OLD Bear looked all around the room to see whether any paws or ears were showing. It wasn't very tidy.

First he found a sock that he'd lost weeks ago. And then he found at least ten marbles that had rolled underneath things. He even found Cat, who wasn't really lost or hiding, and Cat helped him look for the others. But he couldn't find them.

'It's no good,' he sighed. 'I can't find any of you. I can only find things I'm *not* looking for. Can we tidy up a bit and then start again?'

ONE by one the other toys wriggled out of their secret hiding places. All of them, that is, except Little Bear.

'Where's Little Bear?' asked Bramwell Brown, but nobody seemed to know.

'Well he can't be far away,' said Old Bear. 'Let's give him a shout.'

They all climbed up on a chair and called 'LITTLE BEAR' so loudly that they made themselves jump and almost fell off. Duck prodded all the cushions with his beak to see whether Little Bear was underneath, and Bramwell peered under the bed.

'HE could be under here,' he said.

'Well, I'm not going to look,' said Duck. 'It's dark and dusty.'

'Oh, I'll go,' said Rabbit. 'It's just like a tunnel and I love tunnels.' He was just about to dive under the bed when Bramwell grabbed him by the tail.

'Wait a minute, Rabbit,' he said. 'I'll give you the end of this string and then you won't get lost because we'll all be on the other end.'

WITH the string tied round his middle,
Rabbit bounded into the darkness.
The others waited and watched.

Suddenly the string gave such a jerk that Duck
fell on his beak.

'He's here, he's here!' squeaked Rabbit.
'I'm holding on to him, can you pull us out?'

All together they pulled hard on the string and
out popped Rabbit, tail first, clutching not Little
Bear but...

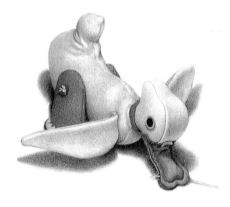

...a fluffy slipper!

'Oh,' said Duck, looking down at the slipper,
'I don't think that's Little Bear.'

'Of course it's not,' said Bramwell. 'He never
looked like that.'

'It *felt* like Little Bear,' said Rabbit.

'It's not your fault, Rabbit,' said Old Bear, kindly.
'You were very brave to go in there on your own
and I'm sure Little Bear will turn up soon.'

'I bet he won't,' said Duck, still gazing at the
slipper. 'He's probably wandered off and is miles
away by now.'

'Rubbish!' said Bramwell.
'I expect he's just stuck
in something. We must
keep looking.'

I think we should make a poster saying "This bear is lost", with a picture of Little Bear on it,' said Old Bear. 'Then all the toys will know who we're looking for.'

The animals all fetched the painting things and Bramwell sat and painted a picture of a small bear in red trousers that did look quite a bit like Little Bear. There wasn't really enough room to write 'This bear is lost', so they just made him look a bit sad and hoped that everyone would know what it meant.

JUST to make sure, Bramwell called all the other toys together and explained what had happened. They all wanted to help and, within minutes, everyone was searching.

They rolled up rugs and climbed up curtains. They jumped into drawers and turned out toys. They peered behind plants and rummaged through rubbish.

They felt as though they'd searched through the whole house but still there was no sign of Little Bear.

'PHEW, I'm tired,' said Bramwell Brown.

'And I'm hungry,' said Duck.

'Well,' said Old Bear, 'everyone has worked very hard and I think we all deserve our picnic. When we've eaten we'll start looking again.'

He led the way to the picnic basket that he'd packed in the morning and lifted the lid.

'There,' he said proudly. 'What do you think of that?'

THE animals all peered inside. But what they saw was not what they had expected to see.

There, lying tucked up under a tea cloth, fast asleep and looking very full, was Little Bear.

'Well, well!' gasped Bramwell Brown.

'Hmm, we seem to have found a bear and lost a picnic,' said Duck, staring at the crumbs that covered Little Bear.

'It's a good thing I made too much then,' said Old Bear. 'There's still plenty left for us.'

Bramwell Brown lifted Little Bear out of the basket and gave him a big hug.

'Come on everyone,' he called, 'picnic time!'

CAREFULLY, they dragged the basket bumpety bump down the stairs and out into the garden.

'This looks like a good place for a picnic,' said Old Bear, spreading the cloth out under a tree.

They had a wonderful feast, finishing every crumb in the basket. Then they stretched out in the sun to rest.

'I know,' said Little Bear, suddenly leaping to his feet, 'let's have *another* game of hide-and-seek.'

But there was no reply. Leaning against the tree and full of food, all the other toys were fast asleep.

Original 'Little Bear'
painting by Owen Hissey

First published in 1989

5 7 9 10 8 6 4

Jane Hissey has asserted her right under
the Copyright, Designs and Patents Act, 1988
to be identified as the author of this work

First published in the United Kingdom in 1989 by
Hutchinson Children's Books
Random House, 20 Vauxhall Bridge Road, London SW1V 2SA

Random House Australia (Pty) Limited
20 Alfred Street, Milsons Point, Sydney,
New South Wales 2061, Australia

Random House New Zealand Limited
18 Poland Road, Glenfield
Auckland 10, New Zealand

Random House South Africa (Pty) Limited
PO Box 337, Bergvlei, South Africa

Random House UK Limited Reg. No. 954009

A CIP catalogue record for this book
is available from the British Library

ISBN 0 09 176408 4

Printed in Hong Kong